W9-ATG-724

Zigzag Zoom

ZIGZAG KIDS

OTHER BOOKS
IN THE ZIGZAG KIDS SERIES

Number One Kid

Big Whopper

Flying Feet

Star Time

Bears Beware

Super Surprise

Sky High

PATRICIA REILLY GIFF

Zigzag Zoom

illustrated by

ALASDAIR BRIGHT

WENDY
LAMB
BOOKS

This is a work of fiction. Names, characters, places, and incidents either are the product of the author's imagination or are used fictitiously. Any resemblance to actual persons, living or dead, events, or locales is entirely coincidental.

 Published in the United States by Wendy Lamb Books, an imprint of Random House Children's Books, a division of Random House, Inc., New York.

Wendy Lamb Books and the colophon are trademarks of Random House, Inc.

Visit us on the Web! randomhouse.com/kids

Educators and librarians, for a variety of teaching tools, visit us at RHTeachersLibrarians.com

Library of Congress Cataloging-in-Publication Data
Giff, Patricia Reilly.
Zigzag zoom / by Patricia Reilly Giff ; illustrated by Alasdair Bright. — 1st ed.
p. cm. — (Zigzag kids ; #8)
Summary: When the Timpanzi Tigers challenge the Zigzag Zebras to a race, Gina worries because she knows she is not a fast runner, but the whole school seems to be counting on her to win.
ISBN 978-0-385-74275-7 (hardcover) — ISBN 978-0-375-99075-5 (lib. bdg.)
ISBN 978-0-307-97704-5 (ebook) — ISBN 978-0-307-97703-8 (pbk.)
[1. Racing—Fiction. 2. Ability—Fiction. 3. Schools—Fiction.]
I. Bright, Alasdair, ill. II. Title.
PZ7.G3626Zig 2013
[Fic]—dc23
2012010179

Printed in the United States of America
10 9 8 7 6 5 4 3 2 1
First Edition

Love to Ryan, Dylan, and Kaylee Grigo
—P.R.G.

• • •

To baby Minla—welcome to the world!
I'm sure you'll be reading in no time
at all!
—A.B.

Yolanda

Sumiko

Charlie

Destiny

Gina

Mitchell

Habib
Clifton
Trevor
Beebe
Angel
Peter

CHAPTER 1

MONDAY

Gina rushed out of her classroom. It was time for the Zigzag Afternoon Center.

She flew down the stairs. Then she went up to the top again and skipped down.

She wanted to hear the bells that jangled on her new white sneakers.

Terrific!

All day, everyone had heard her coming.

Too bad her sneakers were still a little stiff.

She sang a song in a deep voice. *"Toodle-oodle-ooo."*

She was going to be an opera singer when she grew up.

Probably in thirty years!

Hey. What was that?

She stopped at the bottom step. She saw a huge red sign:

HELP!

Where should she go to help?

The lunchroom?

The art room?

The gym?

She raised one foot. She jangled the bell. Maybe she should run right out of there.

Help herself!

No, she couldn't do that.

She heard someone jumping down the stairs. It was her friend Sumiko.

Sumiko was a great jumper.

Sumiko stopped. "Neat bells on your sneakers," she said.

“Thanks. But did you see this?” Gina pointed to the HELP! sign.

“Uh-oh,” Sumiko said. “Someone’s in trouble.”

“But who?” Gina said.

They looked down the hall. “I’ll go one way,” Gina said. “You go the other.”

"Run like the wind," Sumiko said as she took off.

Gina ran faster than she ever had before. Her sneakers slapped up and down. Her bells jingled.

She dashed around Mrs. Terrible Thomas. The cat had sneaked into school again.

But where was everybody else?

She took a quick look in the lunchroom as she went by.

No one was there.

No wonder!

The snack was that red soup with lumps.

She sped on. She was out of breath.

She heard something. It was coming from the gym.

Ramón, the college helper, was blowing his whistle.

Whew, it was loud and screechy.

Maybe Ramón needed help.

How could she help Ramón? He was huge. He was the best basketball player in the Zigzag Afternoon Center.

She pictured Ramón down on the floor. He'd broken a toe. Two toes.

She'd have to drag him all the way to the nurse's office.

She headed for the gym door.

Gina heard a step behind her. She looked over her shoulder. "I can't stop," she called. "I'm trying to save someone's life."

It was her friend Beebe.

"Whose life are you saving?" Beebe asked.

"I don't even know," Gina said.

She heard Ramón's whistle again.

She threw open the gym door.

Almost everyone was there.

What was going on?

People were stamping their feet on the shiny gym floor.

Sumiko came in after her. "Whew," she said. "Nothing's happening down the hall."

Ramón was standing in the middle of the gym.

No broken toes.

He wore a striped suit.

He looked like . . .

A huge zebra!

"Are you ready to help?" Ramón yelled at the top of his lungs.

"Ready!" everyone shouted.

"I'm ready," Gina called.

But how could she help?

She had no idea.

CHAPTER 2

STILL MONDAY

"Take a seat, everyone," Ramón called.

Gina was glad to take a seat. She was worn out from running down the hall.

She climbed to the top of the bleachers. It was the only place she could find.

She just missed Angel's toes.

"Sorry," she said.

She just missed Yolanda's fingers.

"Hey, watch out," Yolanda said.

"Sorry," Gina said again.

At least everyone could see her new sneakers with the bells.

It was worth going all the way to the ceiling.

Mitchell and Habib made room for her. They were good friends.

"Careful," Habib said. He held a paper cup. It was filled with that red soup with lumps.

Gina squeezed onto the bench. She squeezed carefully.

Destiny was right behind her. She squeezed in, too.

"I'm thinking about winning," Habib said.

Winning what? Gina thought. Maybe a hundred dollars. They'd divide the whole thing up. Her share might be five dollars.

Not bad. She already had four nickels and four pennies.

She was saving for a birthday present for Grandma Maroni. A look-like-real diamond ring.

"We'll have to work hard," Mitchell said.

Gina nodded. She'd certainly try.

"Here's the thing," Ramón said from the floor.

Everyone was quiet.

"We've been invited to the Timpanzi School on Smith Street," Ramón said. "The Timpanzi Tigers want to race . . ."

"The Zigzag Zebras," Peter Petway called out.

"That's us," Sumiko said.

"Right," said Ramón. "Can we do it?"

Everyone was yelling, "Yes!"

"We'll have to practice hard," Ramón said. "The race is on Saturday."

Gina took a breath. She'd had enough running for one day.

She wasn't good at running, she knew that.

"Peter Petway is the best runner in the Zigzag Afternoon Center," Mitchell yelled.

"Sumiko is the fastest runner I ever saw," Yolanda called.

Beebe raised her hand. She stood up on tiptoes.

"No," she yelled.

Everyone looked up at Beebe.

Gina hoped she wouldn't fall off the bleachers.

"I know who the best runner is," Beebe said.

Gina looked around.

Who could it be?

Beebe pointed. "It's Gina. I saw her run down the hall. She was fast as a mountain lion."

Destiny gave a little sniff. "I'm fast, too," she whispered.

Everyone turned to look up at Gina.

She didn't know what to do. She gave a wave.

"We're counting on you," Beebe said.

Gina stared at her sneakers.

She didn't want to be counted on. She was slow as a turtle.

Ms. Katz stood up. She looked worried. "We have a problem. We have no money for a bus."

Ramón nodded. "We don't want to walk twelve blocks before the race."

Habib took a sip of soup. "We need big bucks."

Gina raised her hand. She had a good idea. But no one saw her skinny arm in the air.

She kept her hand up, even though it was ready to fall off.

Mrs. Farelli stood up next to Mrs. Katz. "We could have a bake sale," she said.

"Hey," Destiny yelled. "That's what I was thinking."

Gina jiggled her sneakers a little. Sometimes Destiny thought too much!

Gina waved her hand harder.

No one paid any attention.

Mitchell called out, "We could have games. The winner could dunk Mrs. Farelli in a pot of water. I saw something like that on television."

"Great idea," Habib said.

Mrs. Farelli didn't look happy about being

dunked. "I don't think so," she said. "How about selling cookies?"

At last Ramón called on Gina. "Go ahead," he told her.

Gina stood up.

The top of the bleachers was high. Too high.

She hoped she wasn't going to fall all the way down to the gym floor.

She held on to Habib's shoulder.

"We could have someone sing opera," she said. "We could sell a million tickets. Everyone would come."

She opened her mouth wide, ready to sing.

"We don't have any opera singers," Destiny said.

"Well . . ." Gina felt herself teetering.

She held on to Habib a little harder.

"Watch out for my soup," Habib yelled.

"Yeow!" Gina jumped to get out of the way.

Not fast enough.

A bloop of soup spilled out of the cup. It landed on one of her new sneakers.

"Keep thinking, Zigzag Zebras," Ramón said.

How could she think with a bloopy sneaker?

"Don't forget," Ramón went on. "We have to practice running. We have to win!"

Everyone clapped.

Habib gave Gina a poke. "You'll be out front!" he said.

"That's the way, Gina," Mitchell yelled.

"Gina's the best," called Yolanda.

Gina took a breath.

How did she get into this mess?

CHAPTER 3

TUESDAY

Gina stared out the window of the Afternoon Center. Sumiko stared with her.

It was raining.

Pouring.

Was that thunder?

Today Gina loved the rain.

She even loved the crackle of thunder.

She rubbed the window. "We can't practice today," she said.

"I bet you feel sad," Sumiko said. "You're such a great runner."

Gina opened her mouth. She wanted to tell Sumiko the truth. But Mrs. Farelli was clapping her hands. "Everyone to the gym, please."

Uh-oh, Gina thought.

She went down the hall with Sumiko.

Ramón was wearing his zebra suit again. "We have to limber up," he called. "Five to a row."

Gina stood in an all-the-way-back row.

It was a great row.

She was the only one in it.

No one could see if she was limbering up or just hanging out.

"One, two, three, four," Ramón yelled. "Jump right up, off the floor."

Gina gave a little jump.

Her not-so-white sneakers were still stiff. But the bells jingle-jangled.

Yolanda was jumping in front of her. "I can hear you, Gina," she said. "You're a good jumper."

Gina swallowed.

"One, two, three," Ramón called. "Raise each knee."

Gina raised her knee one inch.

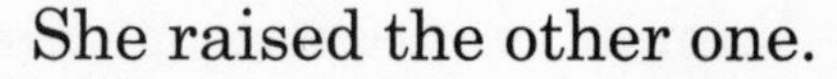

She raised the other one.

Ramón called *one, two, three, four*s and *one, two, three*s a hundred times.

At least.

Gina took a step back.

She took another.

She backed herself right out the gym door.

She leaned against the wall.

How could she race against the Timpanzi Tigers?

And what if she had to walk twelve blocks first?

She'd be lying on the sidewalk like a dead ant with its feet in the air.

First things first, she told herself. *Think of a way to get bus money.*

And then she had an idea.

She went to the lunchroom.

The lunchroom lady was sitting in a chair in the kitchen. She was wearing slippers.

"On my feet all day," the lunch lady said.

Gina nodded. She didn't want to be on her feet all day, either.

"I have a get-money-for-the-bus idea," she told the lunch lady.

"Good girl."

"Grandma Maroni showed me how to make pretzels," Gina said. "They're easy."

"You're right," said the lunch lady. "Great idea."

Gina smiled.

But then the lunch lady had to spoil it. "I hear you're a terrific runner," she said. "You're the one who will beat the Timpanzi Tigers."

"Was that the going-home whistle?" Gina backed out the lunchroom door.

She was doing a lot of backing out today, she thought.

She went to stand in the girls' room for a while.

She might have had a great idea, but she was still a horrible runner.

She opened her mouth. She sang a little opera to herself. *"Ah, ah, ah . . ."*

It was much better than limbering up.

CHAPTER 4

WEDNESDAY

Today the Afternoon Center was going to bake pretzels.

"In between, try running in place," Ramón said.

He took a few steps to show them.

Fast steps!

Gina took a few running steps in place, too.

Very few.

Maybe two or three.

Then she marched down the hall.

She slid into the lunchroom.

Sumiko and Beebe were right behind her.

Mitchell and Habib came in next. So did Clifton, a kindergarten kid.

A minute later, everyone was there. It was snack time.

Bowls of apples were on all the tables.

The lunch lady poked at her cook's hat. "Are you ready to bake pretzels?"

"I'm ready," Clifton said.

Gina could hardly hear him.

Everyone was chomping on apples.

"We'll bake pretzels today," the lunch lady said. "We'll sell them tomorrow."

Habib frowned. "Maybe we could eat a few. Keep our strength up for running."

"We have to sell every single one," Destiny said.

They all went into the kitchen. It was ten times bigger than Gina's kitchen at home.

But what was that noise?

It sounded like a horse galloping.

Gina tried to hear. But the lunch lady was ready to bake.

There was no time to think about horses in the Zigzag Afternoon Center.

Making pretzels was fun.

It was easy.

Not like running all over the world.

In five minutes the dough was ready.

They rolled pieces into snakes. They curved the snakes around, head to tail.

The snakes curled up near each other on the trays.

Mitchell poured salt on them.

The lunch lady slid the trays into the oven.

But what was that noise?

Pounding.

Galloping.

"Do you hear ponies in the hall?" Sumiko asked.

Everyone nodded.

"Yes, ponies!" Gina said.

Destiny said, "Don't think of ponies. Think of all the money we'll make. A dollar a pretzel."

"Maybe two dollars," Mitchell said.

"Well, maybe five cents," said the lunchroom lady.

"I'm going to call my pretzel Snakey," Clifton whispered to Gina. "And I don't want to sell him. I'd like to keep him forever."

"I wish I could eat mine," Habib said. "It's too neat to sell."

Gina hated to sell hers, too. It looked like a poor little snake.

How could someone bite its head off!
Outside the door, the galloping came again.
But this time, there was a crash!
A gigantic crash!
They rushed outside.
It was Peter Petway.
He was on the floor.
His foot was up in the air.

"I was running around the hall," he said. "I was practicing."

"Like a horse," Gina said.

"Like a pony," Clifton said.

Peter looked at his foot. "I think I sprained my ankle."

"Oh, no," said Beebe. "He was our best runner after Gina."

Gina shook her head. "Sumiko's the best," she said.

Sumiko really was the best. Gina knew that.

But no one was listening.

They were helping Peter to the nurse's office.

"I'm not—" Gina began again.

"Not going to give up, right?" Beebe said.

"I guess so," Gina said.

CHAPTER 5

THURSDAY

Everyone lined up in the gym.

Everyone but Peter. He was home with his foot up on a pillow.

"Don't forget," Destiny said. "We have pretzels for sale. They will be on the hall table."

"A quick stop for pretzels," Ramón said. "And then we're going to run."

Gina quick-stepped down the hall.

She could see a little pretzel dough on her almost-new red-bloop sneakers.

Too bad they were still stiff as boards.

And another thing. Her pretzel wasn't on the hall table.

It was tucked inside her pocket.

She'd taken a tiny bite yesterday. She just couldn't resist.

Now her pretzel was missing a little bit of his tail.

The lunch lady was setting up the table. She posted a sign: PRETZELS—5¢ EACH.

"I could help," Gina said.

"Good girl," the lunch lady said. "Take the tray from the lunchroom. Bring it out."

Gina went into the lunchroom.

Clifton was bent over the tray of pretzels.

She knew what he was doing. He was sneaking a pretzel off the tray.

"Hey," she said.

"I don't have any money," he said. "But I don't want anyone to eat this guy."

Gina nodded. She took the rest of the pretzels out to the hall.

There was something she could do.

She reached into her pocket. She took out her pretzel.

She slid it onto the tray.

She heard a noise behind her. It was Destiny.

"Eeeeuuu," Destiny said. "Did you just put that half-eaten pretzel on the tray?"

Gina had money in her pocket. Her life savings.

Four nickels, four pennies.

"I am buying pretzels," she said.

She tried to count.

How many pretzels could you buy for four nickels and four pennies?

It was too much to think about.

"A pretzel for me and a pretzel for Clifton," she said. "The rest is for the bus."

"Great girl," said the lunch lady.

"Thanks," Clifton said. "You're the best."

Beebe nodded. "I know you're going to win the race. And now you're even helping with the bus."

Gina tried to smile.

She went down the hall.

Sumiko tapped her on the arm. "I'm glad you're a fast runner," she said.

"I'm really not," Gina said. "Not like you."

Sumiko smiled. "Sure you are. Everyone knows it."

"You're the best," Gina said.

Sumiko shook her head. "I love to run. But I

can't race that day. It's my uncle Kiyo's birthday. We're going to his house."

"Oh, no," Gina said.

Sumiko looked ready to cry. "His house isn't far from the Timpanzi School. My cousin Satako goes there. We're in the same grade."

Sumiko wiped her eyes. "We're counting on you to win."

What next! Gina thought.

Now they were going outside to run.

In the gym, Ramón blew his whistle. "Here's what we'll do," he said. "We'll run around the schoolyard. We'll go down the block. We'll cross over to Elm Street."

That wasn't such a good idea, Gina thought. Suppose the whole Afternoon Center was run over?

She raised her hand. "What about cars? What about trucks?"

Destiny sniffed. "Only about two cars pass Stone Road every day. And I've never seen a truck."

“Mrs. Farelli and I will stop the traffic anyway,” Ramón said. He tooted his whistle. “Ready?”

“Get set,” called Mrs. Farelli.

“Go!” called Ramón.

They ran in a pack around the schoolyard.

Huff! Huff!

Jake the Sweeper was leaning on his broom. He raised one hand and waved.

They reached the gate. They ran down the street.

Mr. Oakley stood in front of his house. He was holding his kitten. “Go, Zigzag Zebras,” he called.

Huff! Huff!

Sumiko was pulling ahead.

Next to Gina, Destiny was saying, “Nothing to it, right?”

Gina couldn’t answer. She didn’t have one breath left.

She stopped to snap the Velcro on her sneakers.

Destiny kept going.

Gina looked up. She was in front of the Sweet Beat Music Store.

She could see a shiny saxophone in the window.

There was a set of drums, too.
"I can't go another step," Clifton said.
Gina grabbed his hand.
They slid into Sweet Beat together.

CHAPTER 6

STILL THURSDAY

Sweet Beat was huge. One aisle had a stack of harmonicas. Another had drums. Still another had banjos.

In back was a shiny black piano. It was a perfect place to hide.

Gina slid in between the piano and the wall.

Clifton slid in next to her. "I run like a turtle," he said.

"It's all right to be a turtle in kindergarten," Gina told him.

"Really?" Clifton looked happy.

Someone began to play the piano.

Gina knew that song.

It was the great thump-thump kind.

She couldn't help it. She had to thump-thump sing along with it.

First she whisper-sang. *"Da dum-tee-dum!"*

After a while, she forgot about whispering.

She sang in a huge opera voice.

She snapped her fingers.

She slammed her red-bloop-pretzel-dough-still-stiff sneakers together.

The bells jingled.

The piano player kept playing until the end of the song.

He stood up. "Hey, Gina," he said. "Hey, Clifton."

It was Mr. Sarsaparilla, the music teacher at the Zigzag Afternoon Center.

He didn't seem surprised to see them hiding behind the piano.

Not as surprised as Gina was to see him!

"How come you're here?" she asked.

"I like music," he said. "I play happy music when I'm sad. I play peppy music to pep myself up."

He played a quick *ta-tum*!

"How did you know it was me?" Gina asked.

“I’d know your singing anywhere,” he said.

“It’s loud,” Clifton said.

“Yes,” said Mr. Sarsaparilla. “That’s the best part of Gina’s singing.”

“We’re here because—” Gina began.

“I’m a turtle,” Clifton cut in.

“Me too,” said Gina.

Mr. Sarsaparilla smoothed down his mustache. “Really?”

He played another *ta-tum* on the piano.

He sat back. For a moment, he didn't say anything.

Gina and Clifton didn't say anything either.

They listened to someone playing a clarinet.

Gina opened her mouth. She told Mr. Sarsaparilla about racing the Timpanzi Tigers.

She told him about the no-bus-money problem.

She even told him about the pretzel without a tail and spending her life savings.

It felt good to tell all that.

Mr. Sarsaparilla was a great listener. He kept bobbing his head up and down.

His mustache bobbed, too.

Gina heard pounding footsteps.

"Oh, no," Clifton said. "The runners are coming back."

"We have to go," Gina told Mr. Sarsaparilla. "We'll run in place to limber up. Then we'll duck out of the store. We'll catch up to the end of the line."

“Good idea,” said Mr. Sarsaparilla. “Come see me in the music room at the Afternoon Center. We’ll talk about turtles and music.”

Gina squeezed out from behind the piano.

Clifton squeezed out, too.

They ran in place.

Two small, quick steps.

They ducked out the door.

They slid in at the end of the line of runners.

Sumiko was halfway up the block.

What a great runner she was! Too bad she had to visit her uncle Kiyo on Saturday.

"No one saw us," Clifton whispered.

"That's because we're falling behind again," Gina said.

There was something in the back of her head, though.

What was it?

Something important to think about.

The runners raced down the hill.

The school was up ahead.

Gina turned in at the gate.

She was still thinking.

CHAPTER 7

FRIDAY

Gina went down the stairs. She headed for the window.

It had been cloudy all day.

She crossed her fingers.

If only she'd see rain!

Too bad.

Just a bunch of white clouds.

They'd be running all over the world again today.

She looked down at her sneakers.

There was a red bloop on the right one. Pretzel dough was on the left.

And last night she'd dropped green toothpaste on both of them.

Her sneakers didn't look new anymore.

They still rubbed against her ankles, though.

And she was still trying to think about that important thing!

"I have bad news," someone said behind her.

It was Yolanda.

Gina crossed her fingers behind her back. Maybe they wouldn't run today.

"Would you mind not running today?" Yolanda asked.

Gina shook her head. She tried not to smile.

But Yolanda *was* smiling. "You're the best runner. You don't need to practice."

"I'm not the best," Gina said.

She could see Yolanda didn't believe her.

"Someone has to help the lunch lady make cookies," Yolanda said. "It's for bus money."

"I'll do it," Gina said.

"Who else could help?" Yolanda asked.

"Clifton," said Gina. "He runs just like me."

Yolanda looked surprised. But she went down the hall. "I have to practice every minute," she said.

Gina found Clifton. "No running today," she told him.

Clifton jumped in the air. "Cool!"

"We'll make cookies. But we can't eat them," she said. "My life savings are all gone."

"Right," Clifton said.

The lunchroom lady was waiting for them.

She helped them mix up the butter and the sugar. She added the flour and the milk.

"Let me get some vanilla," she said.

She went to her cabinet.

"I like my cookies sugary," Clifton said.

"Me too." Gina wasn't paying attention, though.

She looked down at her sneakers.

A dab of butter had landed on one of them.

A splat of milk had landed on the other.

She looked up.

Clifton was pouring sugar into the dough.

Lots of sugar.

"Stop," Gina said.

The lunch lady came back. She poured in the vanilla.

She put the tray of cookies into the oven.

Gina and Clifton went down to the gym.

Everyone was running in a circle.

"Get your hot cookies," Clifton yelled. "Five cents each. Nice and sugary."

Ramón blew his whistle. "Go ahead," he said.

Everyone dashed for the lunchroom.

Gina didn't dash.

She thought about all that sugar Clifton had added.

She was a little worried.

The lunch lady stood at the door to the lunchroom.

She looked worried, too.

"Sorry," she told everyone. "I don't know what happened. The cookies are flat. They're wet."

She raised her arms in the air. "They're ruined."

Gina didn't look at Clifton.

She didn't look at anyone.

Instead she stared at her sneakers. Was that a drop of vanilla?

She knew what had happened to those cookies.

Too much sugar!

"Uh-oh," Ramón said. "We have only a dollar and forty cents."

He shook his head. "Without the cookie money, we'll have to walk . . ."

"All the way to the Timpanzi School," said Destiny.

CHAPTER 8

STILL FRIDAY

"What can we do?" Destiny asked.

Ramón looked up at the ceiling. "We'll have to practice walking," he said.

"Good idea," said the lunch lady.

"Better than running," Clifton said.

Everyone marched down the hall.

They marched past the gym.

They climbed the stairs.

They waved to Ms. Katz in the library.

Gina marched away from them.
She went down to the music room.
Mr. Sarsaparilla was playing the drums.
Bang-bang.
He hit the cymbals.
Shoom-shoom.
The sound was great.
Gina lifted one foot.
Jingle-jangle.

She lifted the other.

Jangle-jingle.

Gina made up a song to go with the jingling, the banging, and the shooming.

It made her feel a little better.

When the music stopped, she sank into a chair.

She told Mr. Sarsaparilla all that had happened.

"No Sumiko," she said. "No bus."

Mr. Sarsaparilla pulled at his mustache. "That news is not so good," he said.

"And the worst news of all," Gina said. "Everyone is counting on me."

Mr. Sarsaparilla pulled at his mustache again. "You'll have to think hard," he said. "That's what I do when there's trouble."

Gina tried to think hard.

She thought about being in Sweet Beat Music Store.

There was something she'd wanted to remember.

But what?

Mr. Sarsaparilla was playing his harmonica now. It had a *tweet-tweet* sound.

A happy sound.

"That makes me feel a little happy," she told Mr. Sarsaparilla.

"That's why I played it," he said.

Outside she heard footsteps.

All of the Zigzag Afternoon Center was quick-stepping down the hall.

Beebe poked her head inside the door. "I was wondering where you were," she said.

"I was just doing a little singing," she said. "A little . . ."

She tried to think.

She felt her feet in her sneakers.

Her sneakers were a mess. But they felt good.

She told Mr. Sarsaparilla goodbye.

She had to quick-step down the hall with the rest of the Afternoon Center.

If only she didn't have to quick-step all the way to the Timpanzi School.

If only she could think of that important thing.

CHAPTER 9

SATURDAY MORNING

Today was the day of the race!

Everyone lined up in the gym.

Gina wore her best blue sweatsuit with the pink zipper.

She wore her not-new sneakers with the stains and the bells that jangled.

Clifton stood next to her. "Today is the worst day of my life," he whispered.

"Mine too," Gina whispered back.

Ramón blew his whistle. "It's limber-up time," he said. "Then we'll quick-step to the Timpanzi School."

Gina swallowed.

"Are you ready to zoom, Zigzag Zebras?" called Mrs. Farelli.

"I'm ready," Destiny shouted.

"Me too," yelled Habib.

"Right," called Yolanda. She waved a flag she'd made.

Gina and Clifton looked at each other. "Not ready," Clifton whispered.

"No," Gina whispered.

Gina could feel her heart pounding.

Something else was pounding . . . on her arm.

It was Beebe. "Right on, Gina," she said.

Gina gulped. She closed her eyes.

Ramón blew his whistle again. "One-two-three-four," he yelled. "Lift those feet. Walk out the door."

The Afternoon Center marched out the door.

Ramón was up ahead. "Five-six-seven-eight. Let's go, kids. We can't be late."

Mrs. Farelli was in the middle.

Ms. Katz was in the back.

They walked up Elm Street.

They walked down Stone Road.

It was a long walk.

Too long.

Even Mrs. Farelli looked as if she was slowing down.

Gina was not happy!

But then she remembered something! The important thing she couldn't remember before!

She stopped.

Clifton bumped into her. They held each other up for a moment.

Gina thought about Mr. Sarsaparilla.

She thought about his happy music. His peppy music. She thought about his *thump-thump* music.

She began to sing.

First she sang to herself.

Her almost-old sneakers slap-slapped against the sidewalk.

Her bells jingle-jangled.

Clifton began to sing with her.

Thump-thump.

Clifton made believe he had cymbals. *"Shoom-shoom,"* he said.

Mrs. Farelli turned her head. "Great song," she said.

She began to snap her fingers.

Ms. Katz called from the back of the line. "It's a Mr. Sarsaparilla song." She clapped her hands.

Soon everyone was singing.

But Gina was singing the loudest.

Everyone was marching faster.

Mr. Sarsaparilla was right. A peppy song makes you feel peppy.

Gina marched a little faster.

Everyone else was marching faster, too.

It looked as if Charlie had flying feet.

They zoomed along Cromer Road.

Gina put on a burst of speed.

She passed Mitchell and Habib.

She caught up to Beebe.

"I feel peppy," Beebe said. "It's because of your song."

"Listen," Gina told her. "I have bad news."

"What could be bad?" Beebe asked. "We're marching right along. And you're going to win the race for us."

"I'm not a fast runner," Gina said.

Beebe shook her head. "But remember when you were saving someone's life?"

"That was a three-second run."

Beebe opened her mouth. "Do you know what that means?"

"Yes," Gina said. "We're going to lose the race."

"Right," said Beebe.

CHAPTER 10

SATURDAY

The Timpanzi School was up ahead.

A purple banner flew over the door:

WELCOME, ZIGZAG ZEBRAS!

They marched inside.

Dozens of balloons hung from the ceiling.

The Zigzag Zebras were still singing!

Still clapping!

Still stamping their feet!

The gym was filled with people.

Gina saw her mother and father. She saw Grandma Maroni. She even saw Zelda A. Zigzag, the school's first principal.

What would they all think when she came in last?

The Timpanzi Tigers were waving. They looked friendly.

But something else.

They looked worried, too.

"Time to get ready!" the Timpanzi coach called. "Three times around the gym."

Ramón nodded. "We're ready!"

Gina stood in line with the Zigzag Zebras.

Clifton stood next to her.

Then Gina saw the gym door open. "Hey," she said.

"Hey," Destiny said, too.

It was Sumiko!

Next to Sumiko was a girl with a bunch of bracelets.

"This is my cousin Satako," she said.

Satako went to the Timpanzi Tigers line.

Sumiko went to the Zigzag Zebras line. "Uncle Kiyo loves running," she said. "He wants to have the birthday party after the race."

"Ready?" Ramón called.

"Get set," the Timpanzi coach called.

"Go!" they shouted together.

Everyone began to run.

Gina's old sneakers felt great. She sang to herself.

She didn't even feel tired.

She still ran like a turtle.

But she was a fast turtle.

Next to her Clifton was singing, too.

They finished once around the gym.

Sumiko was out in front. But so was her cousin Satako.

They started around the gym again.

Gina was feeling peppy. She was feeling happy.

She knew she wouldn't win the race. But it was fun to run with everyone.

And she was getting faster.

By next year, she might even be at the front of the pack.

Destiny ran next to her. She was singing a *thump-thump* song. "I don't feel tired," she called. "Thanks, Gina!"

Now they were coming to the end of the race.

Who was going to win?

Sumiko and Satako crossed the line at the same time.

"Even Steven!" called Ramón.

"A tie!" called the Timpanzi coach.

Beebe and Charlie came in next!

"Blue ribbons for everyone," the Timpanzi coach shouted.

Everyone sank down on the floor.

Everyone but Sumiko and Satako.

"You're all invited to Uncle Kiyo's birthday party," Sumiko said.

"We're having chocolate cake," said Satako.

"That's the best part of today," Gina said.

"I hope there's not too much sugar," Clifton said.

Gina looked down at her sneakers.

There was just enough room on them for a little chocolate icing!

She gave a hop.

Her bells jingle-jangled.

She sang along: "Yay, Zigzag Zebras! Yay, Zigzag kids!"

PATRICIA REILLY GIFF is the author of many beloved books for children, including the Kids of the Polk Street School books. Several of her novels for older readers have been chosen as ALA-ALSC Notable Children's Books and ALA-YALSA Best Books for Young Adults. They include *The Gift of the Pirate Queen; All the Way Home; Water Street; Nory Ryan's Song,* a Society of Children's Book Writers and Illustrators Golden Kite Honor Book for Fiction; and the Newbery Honor Books *Lily's Crossing* and *Pictures of Hollis Woods. Lily's Crossing* was also chosen as a *Boston Globe–Horn Book* Honor Book. Her most recent books are *R My Name Is Rachel, Storyteller, Wild Girl,* and *Eleven,* as well as the first seven books in the ZigZag Kids series. Patricia Reilly Giff lives in Connecticut.

Patricia Reilly Giff is available for select readings and lectures. To inquire about a possible appearance, please contact the Random House Speakers Bureau at rhspeakers@randomhouse.com.

ALASDAIR BRIGHT is a freelance illustrator who has worked on numerous books and advertising projects. He loves drawing and is never without his sketchbook. He lives in Bedford, England.